I am NOT a princess!

Bethany Burt   Illustrations by Brenda McCallum

Schiffer Publishing Ltd

4880 Lower Valley Road · Atglen, PA 19310

Designed by Brenda McCallum

Type set in Coop Forged / Xiomara

ISBN: 978-0-7643-5212-6

Printed in China

Published by Schiffer Publishing, Ltd.

4880 Lower Valley Road
Atglen, PA 19310
Phone: (610) 593-1777
Fax: (610) 593-2002

E-mail: Info@schifferbooks.com

For our complete selection of fine books on this and related subjects, please visit our website at www.schifferbooks.com. You may also write for a free catalog.

This book may be purchased from the publisher. Please try your bookstore first.

We are always looking for people to write books on new and related subjects. If you have an idea for a book, please contact us at proposals@schifferbooks.com.

Schiffer Publishing's titles are available at special discounts for bulk purchases for sales promotions or premiums.
Special editions, including personalized covers, corporate imprints, and excerpts, can be created in large quantities for special needs. For more information, contact the publisher.

To be yourself in a world
that is constantly trying to make you something else
is the greatest accomplishment.

Ralph Waldo Emerson

"I want to be a beautiful princess!" thought Eliza.

"I'll just put on my favorite princess dress and all my jewelry and gloves. I'll also need my glass slippers and beaded purse."

"Aaah! Now I'm a beautiful princess!"

"Look at me, Mom. I am a beautiful princess!"

"So you are," said Mom.
"Would the beautiful princess like to come
with me to the grocery store?"

"Mom, **princesses** don't shop for food!
They have servants and stuff who make all their food for them,"
Eliza snorted.

"Oh, really?" asked Mom. "I'll have to remember that."

There was a knock at the door. "I'll get it!" Eliza called.
"Maybe it's another **princess** coming to play with me . . .

"or maybe
it's a handsome prince coming to marry me!"

Eliza sagged when she saw her friend Maggie on the steps.
"Hi, Eliza!" said Maggie. "Do you want to ride bikes with me?"

"Princesses don't ride bikes!" said Eliza. "We have horse-drawn carriages that take us everywhere. Besides, I might mess up my beautiful dress."

"Ok, well, I'm going to ride anyway," said Maggie.

"Maybe we'll play another time, when you're not being a *princess* any more."

"Humph!" said Eliza.

"Oh, I'm a beautiful princess!

"That's me! Princess Eliza!"
Eliza twirled and twirled.

Tired of twirling, Eliza thought,
"What else can I do?
I wonder what Spencer is up to."

Her brother was in his room.
"Do you want to play with me,
Spencer?" she asked.

"I'm going to play baseball with Max and Alice," Spencer said, then offered,
"You want to come?"

" Don't you see my gorgeous dress and my fancy jewels?" asked Eliza.

Eliza took off her glove and showed off her ring with a big, sparkly pink gem.

" I can't possibly play a dirty sport like baseball. I am a beautiful princess!"

"Ok, well, we'll miss you!" Spencer said,
leaving Eliza alone with all of her fancy princess stuff.

"Humph!" thought Eliza.
"I wonder what Dad's doing."
Eliza kicked up her heels and danced outside
to find Dad painting the house.

"Hi, Dad.
Do you want to play princess
with me?" asked Eliza.

"I'm busy painting now," he said.
"But I know you love to paint, too.
Do you want to join me?"

"Daaaaad!" wailed Eliza. "Can't you see I'm a beautiful **princess**? I can't possibly help you paint!"

"Well, what can you do then?" Dad asked.

"Um, I can . . .
twirl around and . . . look pretty . . .
and . . . um, and . . ."
Eliza had run out of things to say.

Back inside, Eliza was delighted to discover
her mom was in the middle of one of Eliza's favorite activities.

"What are you doing, Mom?" Eliza asked, excitedly.

"I'm making cookies," Mom replied.

"Yippee!" Eliza said.
"You know I love to make cookies!
Can I help?"

"Eliza, princesses don't cook,"
Mom reminded her.

"They have servants who make
all their food, right?"

"But, Mom,"
said Eliza,
"I can't ride my bike!
I can't play baseball!
I can't paint!
I can't go food shopping
or make cookies!!!
What can I do?"

"I don't know.
What do princesses do?"
Mom asked patiently.

"I don't know," sighed Eliza.
Twirl?
Look pretty?
Nothing really, I guess.

" Hmm, maybe being a *princess* isn't so great after all. "

"I am **NOT** a princess!"

Eliza tore off all her fancy princess stuff
and hopped on her bike.

"Hey Maggie! Wait for me!"

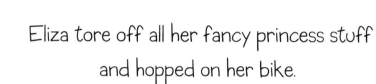

About the Author

Bethany Burt has never wanted to be a princess. As a young girl she loved playing sports and climbing the enormous pine trees that surrounded her home in Wynnewood, Pennsylvania. She missed the princess phenomenon entirely; that is, until her daughter Eliza was born. Bethany has been an advertising, design, and marketing specialist for over twenty years and, like the storybook character, loves to write, draw, paint, and bake cookies. Her two amazing children serve as inspiration for her stories.

About the Illustrator

Even as a little girl Brenda McCallum knew she wanted to bring the world of her vivid imagination into her future work place. As a design professional for over twenty years, she developed compelling and original marketing campaign strategies for corporate clients. Now, as a designer for Schiffer Publishing, she uses her creative passion to help authors leave a legacy of beautiful books that inspire readers to discover new ideas and follow their own adventures of the mind.